HOORAY
FOR GRANDPARENTS' DAY!

by Nancy Carlson

PUFFIN BOOKS

To my grandparents:

Alice and Walter Carlson

Dorothy and Walter Carlson

(Yes they are *all* Carlsons!)

PUFFIN BOOKS
Published by the Penguin Group
Penguin Putnam Books for Young Readers,
345 Hudson Street, New York, New York 10014, U.S.A.
Penguin Books Ltd, 80 Strand, London WC2R ORL, England
Penguin Books Australia Ltd, Ringwood, Victoria, Australia
Penguin Books Canada Ltd, 10 Alcorn Avenue,
Toronto, Ontario, Canada M4V 3B2
Penguin Books (N.Z.) Ltd, 182-190 Wairau Road,
Auckland 10, New Zealand

Penguin Books Ltd, Registered Offices: Harmondsworth,
Middlesex, England

First published in the United States of America by Viking,
a division of Penguin Putnam Books for Young Readers, 2000
Published by Puffin Books, a division of Penguin Putnam
Books for Young Readers, 2002

1 3 5 7 9 10 8 6 4 2

Copyright © Nancy Carlson, 2000   All rights reserved

THE LIBRARY OF CONGRESS HAS CATALOGED THE VIKING EDITION
AS FOLLOWS:
Carlson, Nancy L.
Hooray for Grandparents' Day! / by Nancy Carlson. p. cm.
Summary: Arnie doesn't have grandparents to come to
school on Grandparents' Day, but it turns out he has a lot
of people who can substitute.
ISBN: 0-670-88876-1   [1.Grandparents—Fiction. 2.Schools
—Fiction.] I. Title. PZ7.C21665 Ho 2000 [E]—dc21 99-046237

Puffin Books ISBN 0-14-230125-6

Printed in the United States of America

Tomorrow was Grandparents' Day at Lassie Lower
School, and everyone was busy getting ready.
Everyone except Arnie.

"Hey Arnie, will you help me put up this poster?" asked Harriet.
"Sorry, I have library books to return. Besides, who needs Grandparents' Day?" Arnie grumbled.

When Ms. Childs saw his face she asked, "What's the
matter, Arnie? Didn't you like your books?"
"The books were great," said Arnie, "but Grandparents'
Day is tomorrow and I have no one to bring."

"Hmm . . . why don't you invite a grownup you know well?" said Ms. Childs. "I'm sure lots of grownups would love to be a grandparent for a day."

"That's a great idea!" said Arnie. "I'll ask Mr. and Mrs. Timmer from next door."

Arnie worked on his invitation all day long.

"Whatcha got there, Arnie?" asked Jerry.

"I'm inviting my neighbors to come for Grandparents' Day tomorrow," said Arnie.

"Hi, Arnie! Want to play catch?" Coach Ed asked.

"Sorry, Coach. I have to get home and invite my neighbors to come for Grandparents' Day tomorrow," said Arnie.

Arnie ran all the way home. Past Bill and Dottie's
bakery where he usually got his after-school snack . . .

and past the Paris Dress Shop where Madame Jeanne
always straightened his shirt and smoothed his hair.

When Arnie finally got to Mr. and Mrs. Timmer's house . . .

they were gone!
Now who would he bring for Grandparents' Day?

Arnie thought and thought and thought. But by the next morning he still hadn't come up with someone who could be his grandparent for the day.

At the Paris Dress Shop, Madame Jeanne said, *"Bonjour,* Arnie. Why the sad face?"

"Today is Grandparents' Day at school and I have no one to bring," said Arnie.

"Poor Arnie," said Madame Jeanne as he walked away.

When Arnie got to Bill and Dottie's bakery, Bill said, "You missed your after-school snack yesterday, Arnie. How about a doughnut?"

"No thanks, I'm not very hungry," said Arnie. "Today is Grandparents' Day at school and I don't have anyone to bring."

"Poor little guy," Bill whispered to Dottie.

On his way into school, Arnie saw Ms. Childs.
"Why Arnie, where are your neighbors?" she asked him.

"They're out of town," he said, "so now I don't have anyone to come as my grandparents."

When Arnie got to class there were grandparents *everywhere*.

"Arnie, where are your grandparents?" whispered Harriet.
All at once there was a knock at the door.

It was Bill and Dottie! "Hiya, Grandson!" said Dottie.
"How about some doughnuts for everyone?" asked Bill.
Then there was another knock . . .

and in came Madame Jeanne!
"*Bonjour*, Arnie! It is I—your *grandmère*."
Before Arnie could say anything,

in came Ms. Childs, Coach Ed, and Jerry!
"We heard our grandson needed us," said Jerry.

Harriet nudged Arnie.
"So what do you think of Grandparents' Day *now*?" she asked him.

Arnie looked around the classroom.

"I never knew a kid could have so many people care about him," he said. "Hooray for Grandparents' Day!"